JIMMY REES

HOLIDAY SORTED!

ART BY **BRIONY STEWART**

affirm press

'WHAT WILL WE DO ON OUR **HOLIDAY,** DAD?'

asked Lenny.

'Lots of **FUN** things with Nanna and Pop,'
said Dad. 'We have to go soon, so leave anything
you need at the front door and I'll pack it in the car.'

'Kids, you heard Dad! We're leaving in **15 MINUTES**.'

'And make sure you go to the toilet, it's going to be a long drive,' said Mum.

'OK!' said the kids.

The kids went to the toilet one by one.

'NICE WORK!'
said Mum.

'GOOD STUFF!'
called Dad.

'EXCELLENT!'
said Mum and
Dad together.

They placed their favourite things at the front door, ready for Dad to pack.

They even helped Dad make room for **EVERYTHING**.

'CAN WE GO ON HOLIDAY NOW?'

asked Lenny.

'Safety first!' said Mum.

'Last chance before we set off. Are we sure we've packed everything?' asked Dad.

'WAIT! WHAT ABOUT LEXI?'

asked Lenny.

Dad and Lenny went
back in for Lexi.

Mum dashed back
in for the snacks.

'WE CAN'T LEAVE YET, MY SNORKEL IS **BROKEN!**'

Dad fixed
the snorkel.

'I THINK MACK NEEDS TO GO TO THE TOILET AGAIN!'

Mum and Mack went back inside.

'NOW I NEED TO GO AGAIN!'

'Be quick, we need to beat the traffic!' said Dad.

Dad raced back indoors.

'WE'RE OUT OF SNACKS, MUM.'

Mum joined
Dad inside.

'Back in the car, kids. It's time to go on holiday!' said Dad.

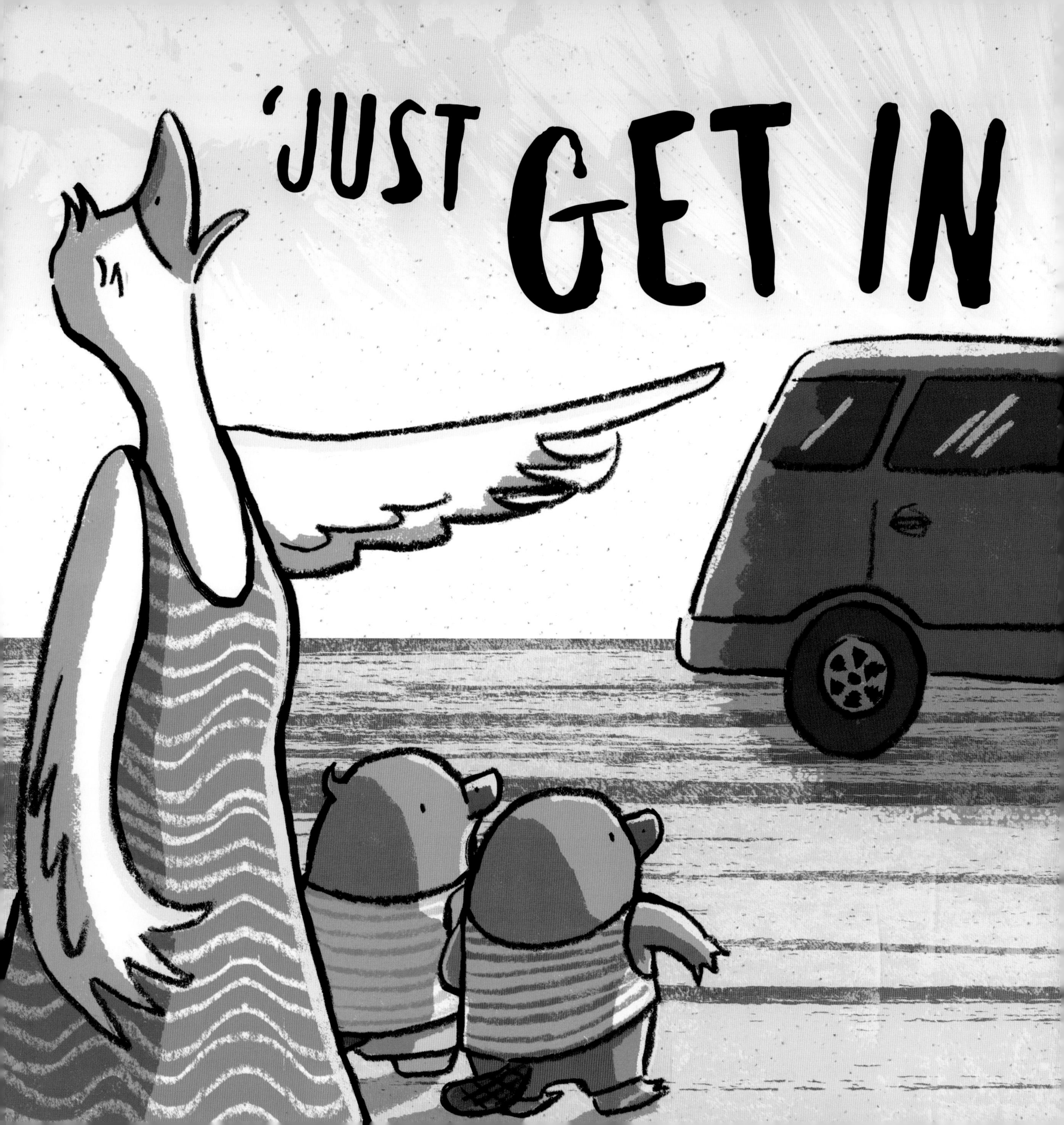
'JUST GET IN

Some time later ...

'Did you pack **ANYTHING** for the holiday?' asked Pop.

'Yep: the kids!' said Mum and Dad.

'Enjoy,' added Dad, with a wink.

Dedicated to my awesome family
and all the beautiful memories made
on holidays ... even though we need a
holiday after the official holiday!! 😌

– JIMMY REES

For my summer holiday peeps,
the effort is always worth it.

– BRIONY STEWART

**affirm
press**

First published by Affirm Press in 2023
Boon Wurrung Country
28 Thistlethwaite Street
South Melbourne VIC 3205
affirmpress.com.au

10 9 8 7 6 5 4 3 2 1

 A catalogue record for this
book is available from the
National Library of Australia

ISBN: 9781922848048 (hardback)

Cover design by Kristy Lund-White © Affirm Press
Cover illustrations by Briony Stewart © 2023
Internal design by Kristy Lund-White
Typeset in Archer Book by Kristy Lund-White
Printed and bound in China by RR Donnelley